Hell's Press Presents

First paperback edition 2023

ISBN 978-1-7381321-8-8 (paperback)
ISBN 978-1-7381322-7-0 (ebook)

hellspress.com

Fairie Tales

The Pied Piper

COUNT FATHOM

Dedicated to...

... you, who have lost the illusion of being eternal. Who have been thrown into the world, responsible for everything you do, condemned to be free. If only that were the case, life would indeed be a solemn affair.

One wouldn't say so had he a clear view of fate's vacant stare. How little we know of the web that binds us together. How our echo spreads, eternal, changing forever the nature of things. How freedom of choice, if it exists, allows us to pluck at the strings of fate's web. If you're in a knot, it's your own damn doing.

I want to leave, to go somewhere where I should be really in my place, where I would fit in. But my place is nowhere; I am unwanted. And haunted. By Nothingness.

Inspired by Jean-Paul Sartre

Table of Contents

Preface

Finally we've reached the end. Nevermore need you expend the energy to read the Tales. But you will, because you must. Fate's winds have blown your ship this far, and one day you can expect another gust. A hand you've on the tiller and you tinker with the jib, your freedom is a falsehood, fate's most favourite flippant fib. The weather keeps you home one night to avoid a fatal crash. You would've won the lottery, but didn't have the cash the week your numbers turned up right, unaware a victim of fate's mischievous spite.

The Piper is the only man who's free of puppet strings, a luxury quite out of reach

of earth's most potent kings. That's because
he's not a man, but born of fairie blood.
His anger can unlock a force of nature
like a flood. Worst of all for most of men,
he's moral to a fault. Transgress his rules
with caution, for he's not above assault. His
principles are iron clad, but guess them you
cannot. Maybe try a bribe, his acquiescence
can be bought. For fairie blood is avaricious,
vicious, blunt and cold. The Piper can be
blinded by a fair sized pot of gold.

    With this advice to guide you, maybe
luck will see you through. I hope you've
packed a four leaf clover to go with your
horseshoe.

The Pied Piper

Three Blind Mice

Wren, Sparrow, and Lark, three little field mice run through the park. Who is that having a picnic this day? They can't see at all, so which one's to say? Wren smells fresh bread, and Sparrow the meat. But Lark isn't smelling for a day's tasty treat. This one's not foolish, he's hatched a nice plan, as only at the brink of survival we can. Lark sees a blind mouse won't have half a chance of living a year if he can't find his pants. "Diurnal predators, from dawn to the dusk, will hunt us and kill us with wing, claw and tusk. Then others wake up to stalk in the night. A mouse must be always ready for flight."

Wren's a philosopher and explains it like this, "the body is nothing more than an shell. Ourselves are within, the flesh just a husk. Upon death there is nothing you're likely to miss about living, provided you're not cast down to hell."

"Spurn the moment!" Sparrow sputtered, "How dare you do so! We're here but a blink of fate's fearful eye. We swim in the stream, the strong steady flow of a fluid time sweeps us by. So swim while you can! Backstroke and breaststroke, butterfly, free, in life you're the man! But you must seize the opportunity! Lay aside your well made plans. Express yourself within the community. Together we'll be us! So much worry, so much fuss eliminated painlessly, wouldn't you have it thus?"

These mice are formidable, intelligent to boot. But they're starving in the park, and must skulk and rob and loot if they hope to live to see the sun in the east rise over head. Like as not we'll find these mice before the dawn are dead.

Sandbox

Rina roamed in innocence to places far and wide, Gita followed faithfully, bolstered to her side. They came across some boys in play around some balls of glass. But they couldn't understand the meaning of a snake eyes or a pass. Rina wandered on across the endless garden lawn, an helpless unwatched simple girl, a pint sized fearless fawn. She comes across a solemn crowd, a stage, an act, a play. The lead says something dark out loud and scares our girl away. On she goes, across the earth, a wide and open path. She shuffles forward to the slide, beyond the fountain bath. Kids play here too, everywhere. For in Hamelin, all the world's a fair.

What a lovely place you've come to while away an hour! The weather's fine, the girls in shape, the bells ring in the tower. All conspire to still your heart in a pixie poisoned way. For never once there was a town, of fabled lore or nought, that lived a life of peace and grace and quarrel seldom sought. For towns are men, and men are towns, and trouble's always found where funds are tight and hungers bite, there's not enough to go around. For now, though, Hamelin's in the black, the money flows in gobs. She's overrun with customers, they're herded through in mobs. Grain they want, all we can grow. We grow it thick as thieves. If it weren't for rotten politicians, administrative sieves, then Hamelin would be fairie perfect, fine in every way. The people woke to yet another fair and pleasant day.

"Lark! What have you done? You've led us to danger, this plan's not so fun." The mice he'd convinced to get into the bag and be carried back home by this porky old hag. At least so they thought, they were blind after all. But they were quite certain by the voice and no balls. Sparrow, that rascal, burrowed that cave. He's shameless and plucky and lucky and brave. The woman got up and collected her stuff, then she paused for a moment, bends over and huffs. The mice in that moment got into the bag, and are now on their way with this horrible hag.

"We'll live with her, hidden." Lark pleaded his case. "A home and a table, a bed and a bath, an endless supply of her grain. All seasons we'll revel in comfort, not suffering under the rain. We'll be warm and fed just like I said, you'll forget what it's like to complain."

Sparrow's unsure and Wren thinks it's crap. They're both afraid they'll be caught in a trap, or killed with some poison, or stuck on some glue. The ways that mice perish are more than a few. Undaunted, unwavering, Lark grits his teeth, but just to be safe he buries beneath all the stuff this gal carries around in the bag. Things will be fine if his brothers don't nag.

Off they go in a cart, to the porch of a home. A man opens the door, he's holding a comb. He's bald, which is puzzling, but not to his wife. She knows something's wrong with this y chromosome. He can be witty and charming, with a wide pleasant smile. But once he has what he wants you'll get nothing but bile. He'll shout and he'll stomp, if you let him he'll tear at your clothes and your papers, maybe even your hair. Say hello to this man, don't short on the pomp, for standing before you is Hamelin's fat mayor.

"I've been called to the office, I'll be home at five. Make dinner for three, serve oysters alive. I'm bringing a girl, next to me she will sit. She's desperate I sign off on her liquor permit. Be quiet at table, and when you hear me cough, make haste, hurry up, and kindly screw off. You won't like the customs of business like this, for they're traditionally sealed with the gift of a kiss. It's normal, my woman, it's nothing but form. Let's settle this now instead of making a storm in front of the girl. In return I'm gifting her your mother's pearls."

Into the kitchen she heads with a frown. The mice scurry out as she puts the bag down. This is the hard part, they're all in the dark. The two brother's pause, then run after Lark. A tragic undoing, near fatal, mistake. Lark knew no better what direction to take. They all ran after the fat man's wife. She cut off their tales with a carving knife. Have you ever seen such a sight in your life? Three blind mice.

See how they run? Straight out the door in anger and pain. They flee to the forest, but behind leave a stain, a trail of tail blood spilled upon the path, dark and red and menacing, a scent picked up on fast by a pack of three such female rats that never did you see. Horny and aggressive were these dangerous rats. The blind mice all agree. "Revenge we'll seek, for damage done, upon the race of man. And through these horny rats, my brother's we'll show the world we can."

The blind mice mated rats that night,

in an act of angry vengeful spite. The proge-
ny forthcoming are a franken-hateful-fear. If
you happen to run in to one, I advise you to
stay clear. The pack grows ever larger from
a group of three or four to a herd of several
dozen and from thence come even more.
They will eat through all your produce, not
for food but from delight at disturbing your
existence and in adding to your plight. They
hate you, pure and simple, and will haunt
each waking hour. But it's worst at night,
they'll screw you right by eating through the
flour. Grain is Hamelin's commerce, with a
premium for grinding at the mill. The rats
will gorge themselves, Nuck's power slowly binding.

Piper

There was a girl, her name was Kate,
she loved a dwarvish king. Though he wasn't

handsome, tall or strong, she couldn't find a thing he wouldn't do for her, and so good Kate said yes. The fates have long been calling Kate, the good they like to bless.

His world was through a tunnel in a mountain in the east. Kate went through and met that world a dozen times at least, often wishing she could bring to us the dwarf civility. The world of man could not adapt, we hadn't the ability to behave with grace and charm and kindness, all with great humility.

Alas! One day the bridge collapsed between our world and theirs. Fate is fond of giving out and taking each its share. You'll never unravel the spin of the marvel of fate's most mysterious affair. Kate was stuck in our world while the king was on his side, obliging to the law, for on his presence they relied. The hole collapsed, and never more did these two lovers meet. But, of consequence, into our world a Prince I'll have you greet.

A child was born to Kate and, in the turbulence of fate, the boy was tall but underweight, and by the age of nine or eight displayed the queerest piebald trait of the most dashing bright array of clothes in which to robe himself most gay. Happy smiling, twirling in the lilies, styling hair on forest animals that came at his request. For this dwarvish giant prince could lull with song. His very tune would quite arrest your heart and mind and seep into the fabric of your soul until you slept in dreamless slumber, swept upon the wave of tune. To the brink of your destruction you are led like a buffoon.

Piper! He has arrived. How have you survived without his sharp, but cheerful wit? But beware his dwarvish anger, do not

question his resolve. Your transgressions he
won't suffer, misbehaviour not absolve. He'll
kill to punish beyond measure, past considered fit. To fate he is a reaper, causing havoc
in his wake. A fourth is flat, the tempo lost,
and now he's on a break. He alone amongst
the men will plot and set his course, liber-
ated from the fields, the fabric of the force,
the dimensional lines we can't even imagine,
from an unknown unknowable source.

"Mother, dear, you are a saint. I've
loved you all my days. You've tried your best
to train me to be kind in every way. I am,
I'd say, a moral man, by laws I do abide. But
when I see injustice done I won't sit on the
side. Retribution I will have, revenge I will
pursue. Brutal will my vengeance be, not
just a slap or two. Dwarvish law prevents
the crime from happening again by slaying a
genetic line, we want not harmful men. This

law I bring to save us from destructive evil cads. If that means slaying children, well, bring on the little lads. I'll kill the instinct to be bad, believe me that I will. For only I have nerve enough to administer this prophylactic pill."

Kate, she sits in silence. Her thoughts are all her own. Piper is her only child, she loves him to the bone, but his penchant for eugenics Kate, in conscience, won't condone. She knows this is a parting from her one and only son. If he is going to murder, then she is forced the boy to shun. On this last day she counsels him of stain he must beware, for acts of evil in our life, our souls we shred and tear. Even with his dwarvish blood, though he may take great care, a life eternal is not his, "Mortality we share, my son. Farewell." Kate will shed many a tear, I fear, even for the souls in hell.

Where Piper wanders for many a year is, I'm afraid, not certain, not entirely clear. A lack of a man, I think I might see, a teller of stories, a man quite like me. He needs imagination to see aardvarks ski. Or to have human hair growing out of a tree. What would it be like to not have our knees? He likes talking fish and exotic disease. It would be best if he weren't so hard to please.

A pipe Piper found one day. Left behind, as some might say, the owner's demise came an unusual way. At home he was found, in no way was he bound, but he'd eaten an chain anyway. The man, a musician, a poor showing had given, drunk as he was. Piper was driven to address the man thus, "Man! That was bad. I'm frightfully mad, I've paid and you cheated, you foul, thieving cad!"

"Bum luck!", said the man, "sometimes I'm ok. Pay again tomorrow, you'll see me play."

At this Piper went to the man directly and took the instrument from him. In a haunting, ghostly, druid voice, the Piper gentle starts, a pair of alternating bass notes slowly climb the octave chart. Somehow the man begins to feel a grip upon his heart. Up he gets and wanders while the Piper plays the tune. There's the chain, he has it now, and now is not too soon, he stuffs the chain into his mouth and swallows, the foolish buffoon. But he hasn't the slightest chance of escaping Piper's trance, lifted from his pants into a will-less flood from Piper, a gift of his dwarvish blood.

And now our Piper has the pipe. It's his, is as just and good. According to his principles, his coin as well he should, and he does, the Piper, take the man for everything he's got. Dwarvish laws are unforgiving, and the Piper's blood has not forgot. If you think the Piper brutal, I implore you stay away. When you listen to his song compelled you are to him obey. None will stop his purpose, none his path will intercede. You will do as he commands, you'll suffocate or bleed. You'll kill your wife and then your child, you'll mix milk in your rum. You won't know where you're going to or where you're coming from.

The piper plays a soulful tune and life just must respond. It's from the dimen-sions our senses can't see. And that's before knowing our senses deceive. It still is a part of our reality, matter in fields that we just can't perceive. Measure what we can, that's good, but theory must look beyond. It's in the math, our greatest tool. So calculate until you drool! I'll let you stop once you've made a pool.

These other dimensions, beyond com-
prehension, they rarely take act in our own.
Though not impossible, it's not like the
gospels, but go on and think on your own.
I'm not here to tell you what it is you should
think. By god, I'll sure let you put milk in
your drink! But for science and its applica-
tion we should surely pay if we are to utilize
our resources in an even and balanced way.

Long has the piper roamed over the
land. We find him now somewhat grizzled
and tanned by the kiss of the sun and the
touch of the wind, he's not quite as spry
and his hair slightly thinned. Determined
in justice the piper has been, and so it will
be to the end of his life, till death steals this
dwarf and his ethics fuelled strife. And now
you have met, then we're set to continue
past valley, in vale, by river, through forest in

gulley and dale, to the heart of our legend,
our shared fairie tale. Hamelin's in sight for
the piper at last, awaiting fate's die by Piper be cast.

The Deal

Hamelin would be fairie perfect, fine in
every way. The people woke to yet another
fair and pleasant day. But what came next,
the whole affair, is rather difficult to say.
Shame and horror, guilt and cruelty, morals
delicate to weigh. Hamelin's tale is only for
the fairie tale gourmet. The rats come in a
vengeance, retribution to inveigh.

At first they aren't much noticed.
They're seen in ones and twos, caught in
kitchen cellars, or crawling over shoes. The
people start to talk about the problems that
they make. Just what it is that they should
do, what precautions they should take. Some

are laying poison out, some are grabbing
brooms. Cats are hunting everywhere, in
each and every room. It's not enough, the
rats still spread, determined in their doom.
A week goes by, their numbers grow, the
stored grain's getting thin. The fields are
bare, rats ate it all, no harvest's coming in.
Nothing done can stop the rats, and, much
to their chagrin, the town concedes against
the rats they simply cannot win.

The young are in a panic. Their scream-
ing fills the air. The old are much more
stoic, absorbed in silent prayer. Many carry
handkerchiefs to mop a teary face. We'll not
humiliate them in this very special case, for
I would be found sobbing, curled up fetal
on the ground if these vicious rats in masses
came laid siege within my town. Cupboards
barren, money spent, the water's stained and
brown. They chew and gnaw and bite and

claw, they scratch and make a mess. They're everywhere and all at once, a growth we can't suppress. We're on the brink, we're at wit's end, and now I must confess I'm off to drink one with a friend, I do humbly acquiesce.

Jerome the gnome, mayor of Hamelin, sat fat and official, defended by a broad oak mayoral desk. You've met once before, so you know what's in store from this self serving whore. "You lousy, sub intellect, bleating, furred moo! I'm blaming this whole god damn mess upon you! You were cheap and indulgent, you let them begin, and now they're amok! Tell me, where they're not in!? An election is coming, just a twelve-month to go. You're fired! It's all on you. Get me re-elected. I'll find you something new. Now call in those guys that came in from the zoo."

"You there! You guys go round up these

rats. You can use nets, bullets or cats. I don't care what you do and I won't ask you why, but those rats have to go or we're all going to die."

In runs a man with a worried nervous look. In his hand he holds but one sad lonely chewed up tattered book. "It's all that's left! They've come and eaten every single page. Our knowledge, lore and custom gained in struggles over ages gone in days. This infestation must be stopped! Or the mayor's head, off it will be chopped!"

Here comes a girl, a forehead full of furls. So young to be anxious, but she's trying to be brave. "These rats, my lord! Have no respect, they fill each nook and cave within my home and in the street. They cannot decently behave! I've come upon a prayer that the state my soul will save!"

A third shuffles in, this one just a child,

"My tummy is empty, I haven't eaten for a while. No grain, one can't get fed. Can one of you here spare some bread?"

"Out, child, now! That's enough of your complaints." He was pushed out the door and later put into restraints.

"You bastards are staining my triumphant campaign! My career is over and my secrets out! My guilt and my shame! No! I'll not have it. We're stopping this game. Set fire to the buildings. We'll burn the place down!", when in pokes the head of a mysterious clown. Or colourful, one might say. "I'm Piper. I can help, if you'll pay."

"You can? And you will? You'll get rid of the rats? At least from the homes of our voting aristocrats? Piper, my hero, a thousand guineas for you if the promise you offer can be made to come true! I don't mind that you dress like a nance, a rainbow of colours all over your pants. Get out there and get them! These rats you must kill. Come see me after and we'll settle the bill."

They shook on the deal, or was it a bet? The fat hand of the mayor was covered in sweat. He'd rent out his wife to be done with this threat. The Piper accepted. It seemed a fair trade. He'd get rid of the rats and then he'd get paid. Should we hold him responsible for the mess that's been made? Posterity records the horrors he brought. Are they balanced out? Was a moral lesson taught? Was retribution worth it? Is the end sum a nought? A question I will leave not for me but for you, a puzzle, a conundrum, in your leisure to undo.

Hero

Piper walks out in the street with a grin. Money made so easy that it ought to be a

sin. The musician's pipe he fondles as he rais-
es to his chin the stiff hard wooden barrel, so
long loved it's next of kin. On it Piper blows
a mournful, slow and haunting air. A tenor
voice is carried off to all, a sad compelling
prayer. All are in appreciation, most of all
the wicked rats. They come running to a
siren's song, small, furry acrobats.

Gather in wonder as the Piper he plays,
and the rats follow after in a trance or a
daze, the tune reminiscent of a lute or a lyre,
as if one were accompanying a funereal pyre.
Swaying together, in step with the lot, down
through the streets at a fair ratty trot, they
swarm and they clamber, black, brown and
grey, a dense hairy mass, a menacing fray.
Into the forest the tune they obey. Tangled
and winding, through vales they are led.
Past dale over glen, with Piper at the head
of a queue stretching back to the edge of the

town, a horde of these rats in the steps of
our clown.

A lunge and a perry, a feint and a twirl,
the Piper plays faster and spins in a whirl.
The rats, they grow frantic. They chirp and
they hiss. They scream and they cry and they
completely fail to notice as they draw closer
to a stream. Piper climbs in a boat, push-
es off from the shore, away does he float,
rats follow in hordes. The music the piper
continues to play. The rats in a fury, a blind
tense melee climb over each other, a scram-
ble together, a fierce and psychotic sprawl
into the water. Rats drown in hundreds and
in half an hour the stream is dyed red in
the suicide slaughter. The Piper plays softly
now, some rats still linger. But somehow the
impulse to drown oneself stronger! Finally
every last rat meets their maker, or at least
his subordinate front man caretaker.

In a boat in a stream in a river dyed in blood stands our Piper, the hero, our worshipped nancy stud. All the rats are dead, and standing on the shore are many varied villagers trying to ignore the Piper's calls for some assistance. He's forgot the bleeding oars. They're under some dead rats right there the Piper tries to say. The villagers just standing there, not one among them wouldn't swear the Piper spoke a foreign tongue. The villagers depart en masse, the Piper's left alone. Piper pops into the stream with all the floating mess and swears they will atone for their discourtesy.

Let us leave the Piper too, and maximize his rage. We can leave him on his own for at very least a page. We'll call him back if much in need, but I doubt we'll want him now. The town erupts in joyous glee. Proclaim defeat over the gods sent pestilence in

an raucous intoxicated splendour of gender
fluid joy. Let him be her and him do him
while she and he and her are three, and
more there are than I have seen so who am
I to say. You're free to do for you, as is your
due to being with the right to choose the
use of you and your hereditary horn. An-
kle, back, or armpit, cheek, whatever freaks
your beak, for that you shall surely seek. The
people of Hamelin will celebrate the day and
we would be remiss were we not to have a
little peek.

His mouth, her ass, his hand, I'm feint,
the town awakes with much complaint. Let's
rest another day or two and forbid discus-
sion of our immoral milieu. Can you believe
Fred and Annie!? They seemed so nice. Who
knew? Can't say about after, but damn that
was fun. You wouldn't do that in the bright
light of the sun. For all our neighbours'

puritanical mores, give them half a chance
and they're eager to act as whores. That's best
done in the shadow and the dark, anony-
mous, unfettered, unrestrained, and stark.
Did you know the banker is a shameless bot-
tom gay? Or the butcher likes them chubby,
or miss teacher likes ass play? The mayor's
wife gobbles like a rooster, much admired as
she performed. No surprise before too long
a healthy line had formed. We'll keep it just
between ourselves, a secret bit of bliss. I'm
glad to know within us dwells the passion
for a kiss.

A few days slowly pass. Sober enough to
see, Hamelin's not a child, observes the cold
reality that their position isn't mild. Clean
the rooms, and sweep the floor, restore the
fences and the door, set wrong right where
suits you best, you do for you, might I

suggest. And so we should on ourselves rely when Nuck has locked on us her eye. That ancient, evil, toxic witch, blotting colour with her pitch, a fickle fate sews cross-stitch, so harmful yet important which without our experience of love and life would not exist. We can hide from her at times, at others we must run. But face her we must and many times before our time is done. Face her brave and strong and true. Make sure you behave as only you can do, a you that deep inside is well and truly only you.

Hamelin's put to rights as much as could be done. The celebration over for the victory they won. The rats are dead. But through the long cold starving winter can the people and their lives endure? To the mayor the people turn, the fat boy pompous gnome. What has the state prepared for us? You're on the hook, Jerome. At every easy

problem solved they like us to applaud.
Look how wonderful they are! The populace
is awed. But when the Nuck brings darkness to life's game, officials hunt for one to
blame. Not me! It's him! We'll string him up
and set him straight, we'll end his darkness,
you just wait. As long as someone's pun-
ished, right or wrong we'll close the book
on this discordant song. Officials breathe a
sigh of deep relief. A bullet dodged, a fate
escaped, a never will thou be my grief. Look
again at what I've done! Praise me, praise
me! We're I a woman I'd be a nun. And if
I am one, the rules still hold, she wants to
shine like polished gold.

"Hands up, Hamelin for your mayor,
hallelujah, man, I swear you're so lucky that
I was there. The rats would've run you all
out of town."

"Don't forget about our friend,

the clown!"

"I found the right man for the job.
Now take a knee, you filthy mob! Listen up,
I'll tell it straight. Hamelin's in a tricky state.
I said I'd pay that clown a wad, but if I do
we'll all die over the winter." Harken back to
what I said about the kind of tale you would
be fed.

A sudden silence fills the air, a pecu-
liar puzzled presence waits. Eyes cast down
admiring footwear, shuffles, coughs, ungain-
ly gaits. "Nuck him!" yells a voice within
the room, echoed suddenly, to their doom.
"Nuck him!" shouted him and her, "this loss
we simply can't incur. Nuck him!" chanted
hot and swollen faces, fist pumps, dances,
warm embraces. When who should walk in
through the door, but our old friend Piper,
and he's feeling kind of sore.

"The rats are dead. I've done my bit.

Pay me a thousand guineas and we'll be done with it. I warn you I'm not the kind of man to cross. Be grateful for what I've done for you. To betray me will be your loss. Do not act with unconsidered, ill advised caprice. Pay me and I'll move on in peace. "

"Nuck him!" someone mutters, many others make it matter, mouthing "Nuck him!" hot and bothered, and he's bellied out the room. "We cannot fulfill our promise, clown, and compromise ourselves. We'll keep our money and save our skin, you freaky, piebald elf."

Pushed roughly to the street, Piper stumbles on the lawn. An old woman has a broom in hand and chases Piper on. He gets away, she catches up, the gal's chase undeterred. He's round the block three times or more, her fitness is absurd. On one more lap poor granny's finally running out of breath. If she keeps it up much longer this will surely be her death. There's a lesson to be learned from this athletic escapade. Don't just think her old and harmless, pent up anger over decades want be violently repaid. Piper's lean and light and sinewy. He's built for flight and can continue. On he goes for quite a while and finally he's put granny out of sight.

Now he has the pipe. Softly, gently, with great care, the precious pipe he pulls it out, veiny, thick and bare. What will he do, this clownish man? The question's in the air. To his lips the pipe is placed with the grace of the devout. He blows a note, the children twitch while parents' gasp and shout. Then begins in bass note trills, some flourishes, some flattened fifths, some fills, a melody, a gravity is born. Children, children every-where! They drop their toys, they gawk and

stare. And then they follow, closely bound
by spell or charm, to the Piper's sound
throughout the streets, and by the parks,
by every house, and all will join the Piper's
arc, a ship for children in a swoon, swept on
dwarvish waves, a paralyzing tune.

Rita waltzes, skips and bends, copied
faithfully by her friend. They dance to Piper's lilting lead, following merrily, mind and
deed. All through Hamelin do they roam,
past each and every family home. Every
child of every age with light toned eyebrows,
as one might gauge, fell into the same un-
natural, poisoned daze, trapped inside an
inescapable aural maze. They approach the
town square in Piper's merciless hypnotic
haze. And when Piper suddenly ceased to
play, each and every child in Hamelin chose
to blissfully obey.

They drop their arms, their chins are

down, held by Piper's dwarvish charms. Disregard his nancy gown, the sound is what compels the child to be submissively be- guiled. All this while the people filed beside the children on parade, at first bewildered, then concerned, parents huddled sad, afraid. Some try grabbing from the stream their child and tried to stop the dream. Before they've had a breath of thought, the child goes mental once by the parent caught, thrashes, kicks and scrapes and bites and worse yet joined by other vicious little snipes! The parents surrender their hopeless endeavour and must accept failure to our stubborn vigilante, a jurisprudence epicure. The Piper will make the town pay.

In a town courtyard there stands a lean man. He's dressed like a rainbow, he's tall, strong and tanned. He has in his hands a stiff wooden wonder upon which he blows a hypnotic thunder, under the spell of which children do follow. They're standing here now, but they're vacant and hollow. And then comes the vibrating bass from the pipe. The air is electric, the moment is ripe. The Piper, he slithers about on the keys, the children are stirring, increasing degrees. They're turning and spinning, and whirling in place. Faster he plays and the children keep pace. Round and round at a rollicking rate, each child their best can't their appetite sate. Soon they are dripping in pools of their sweat, slipping and falling and twitching, but never capitulating, despite the obvious and terrify- ing mortal threat. On and on the song flies, as Piper's thirst for dwarvish justice never dies.

Rina's a champ, she's there to the last. Gita held strong, but is fading now, fast. Less than one child in ten's going on with the spin. Gita's done well, but now she gives in. Tripping and stumbling in the circles she makes, drooling, unseeing, a belaboured breathing, and cursed with some violent, spasmodic head shakes, and finally, at last, Gita down she does go. She crumples unconscious, an exhausted little doe. Soon the others follow in Gita's demise, but Rina's going strong, to the Piper's surprise!

Rina's spinning circles like an olympic gymnast vet, while the Piper's getting nervous, he's already drenched in sweat. Every child in Hamelin has succumbed to their fatigue, which lights Rina's accomplishment with all the more intrigue. The Piper knows that some like these can fill the hero's role. And here is one to show us all, this defiant little soul. The Piper lays the pipe aside, with emotional effect. He, too, can be made to feel a pure, profound respect for one of ours

who pass his test. The day is hers! He'll let
her rest.

Around the town, in crumpled piles far
spread, are all the children still as statues, for
they were all stone dead. The dwarvish law
he has fulfilled with the countless children
he has killed. An stern, uncompromising,
merciless law to which the Piper clung.
Perhaps a flaw, but so much a part of his
nature that to set it right would be like a
medical procedure that could change his
height. In the world of men, he is a luna-
tic that measures moral transgression with
a misshapen yardstick, a code of ethics far
from the humane politic. A bloodline dwarvish arithmetic that doomed the Hamelin
children for the actions of their parents, in a
retribution archangelic. Except for one, who
carries on. Not for brains was she preserved,
nor beauty, wealth, her parentage or brawn,

but determination. A soul of steel has Rina
here displayed, her dwarvish debt absolved,
and her life deserved.

The End

Acknowledgments

We're all hoping for a loosening of the morally puritan language considered politely acceptable in this day and age. Victorian England would say we've gone to far. Disadvantaged groups lived long in the dark. And now they've seen the public light. The disadvantages go on, of course, but awareness is a wonderful step forward. Now shush up a little. Life is hard. Harder for you, yes, but don't demean my own struggle. And don't shackle my freedom of speech. That's a core value. We want that freedom.

When you mouth off too much about the wrongs done you, and there's a hint of pretense that society owes you your due, whether in opportunity or respect or acknowledgment, populations with whom you would seek to live peacefully are antago-

nized. Whereas they once stood still, neutral,
they now must push back against you or be
moved themselves. You have created a new
opposition. Pity makes suffering contagious,
says a man. I needn't suffer on your account
unless I want to.

Whether you be dwarves or giants,
a limb lost in battle, or fabulously queer,
whatever the difference you see in yourself,
whatever the tribe you will join and under
whose banner you will march, that's great!
I wish you well if you wish me so the same.
Nearly anything is fine. But I'm scratching
at the earth to fill my belly and protect the
meagre scraps a half a life has left me. I'm
not minding about you much. I'd like not
to be forced to mind. I'm tending mine own
garden. I like it nice and trim.

Author

Man evolved a hand from paw and set that hand to writing law. At first our men did pass the test, seeking laws that served us best. Those men are gone, and in their place we've put a sadly selfish race. Preening feathers, beating chest, popular their only quest, their only merit, only aim. What a shame, the way we've structured this important game.

Each new leader, he or she, hopes for immortality. Achieves, he will, this state of grace, when law is but a piece of lace he wears to decorate his face. So write, he does, at a furious pace, as immortality his name does chase.

What have we now? An endless book, as government our freedoms took away from us, by one but one, until that freedom's all but done. Each new rule these fools do write, from our freedom takes a bite. Under his persistent eye, behaviour he will codify until his name in lights does shine, he cares not how the law confines.

Leadership is not a game meant for one to embellish his name. The laws are passed on all of us, and thus with caution and much fuss each new law we should discuss. Limited the law should be, and subject to our inquiry. Challenged often, often won, these laws must also be undone if they are found to me misplaced, if they offend the modern taste. For law is living, breathing too, A law for me may not fit you. Each case is special, each one unique. Each neighbourhood's a legal boutique. The residents quite free to critique a law they see as false antique.

I leave to you the burden, then, of laws to change, of how and when. I suggest you strike down nine in ten, and try your best to find wise men to wield the almighty legal pen.

Hell's Press

In prison does a man reside, but not alone, alas! He tries to get along with all, make way to let them pass. But one can't help to cause some harm in a world that's made of glass. And look here now, the concrete towers encroach upon the grass. Each step a man may wish to make, another will claim trespass. In leisure together, whatever the weather is what we should learn in class. The men who put this place together spent far too much time in mass.